The Would Be Tree

Sonya S. Smith

Illustrations by Donna Grimes

WestBow Press books may be ordered through booksellers or by contacting:

WestBow Press
A Division of Thomas Nelson & Zondervan
1663 Liberty Drive
Bloomington, IN 47403
www.westbowpress.com
1 (866) 928-1240

ISBN: 978-1-9736-2150-8 (sc)
ISBN: 978-1-9736-2151-5 (e)

Library of Congress Control Number: 2018902590

Print information available on the last page.

WestBow Press rev. date: 03/25/2019

WESTBOW
PRESS®
A DIVISION OF THOMAS NELSON
& ZONDERVAN

There once was a seed that wanted to be a plant.

She wasn't sure what kind of plant she would be, but she was sure of one thing: she did not want to be a weed!

She had heard of one called, "The Gardener," who planted seeds and nurtured them into thriving plants. Being impatient though, she decided on her own to plant herself in the first available spot of dirt she could find. She settled in and was reasonably content.

The seed eventually sprouted and became a small plant – not a big plant – but she felt she was doing all right for herself. She received water from time to time and even produced some pretty flowers, occasionally.

The other plants near her seemed
to like what they saw. She tried
to blend in and live in harmony
with all the plants around her.

On the outside, nothing seemed amiss, but underneath she was struggling. Her roots were weak and pitiful. The dirt in which her roots were attempting to grow was not the best. In fact, it was hard and rocky. It allowed her roots enough space just to get by. They could reach enough water to survive, but not enough to grow.

Some days she liked to imagine she was large and strong. On bright sunny days she often caught a glimpse in the distance of the large majestic trees. They stood with their branches stretched towards the heavens and swayed so joyously.

"Wouldn't that be exciting to grow as big as a tree?" she thought.

Oh well; All the other plants around her seemed content enough, so she would be, too. After all, she didn't have it too bad. She had seen some plants turn brown and die. Others never even made flowers, and they seemed happy. And best of all, she wasn't just a weed. Yes, she was definitely a better plant than the others, so she was doing all right.

From time to time, she would see The Gardener strolling through the garden. How she wished she knew him better! She had heard stories of his great abilities to turn tiny little seeds into wonderful plants and could see some of them from where she grew.

It seemed as if he was really unaware of her, though. The area of the garden she had self-planted in was so isolated and lonely. With all his beautiful plants around, would he care about her?

One day, the plant looked up and was surprised at what she saw. It was The Gardener! She knew he was around, but he had never come so close to her before.

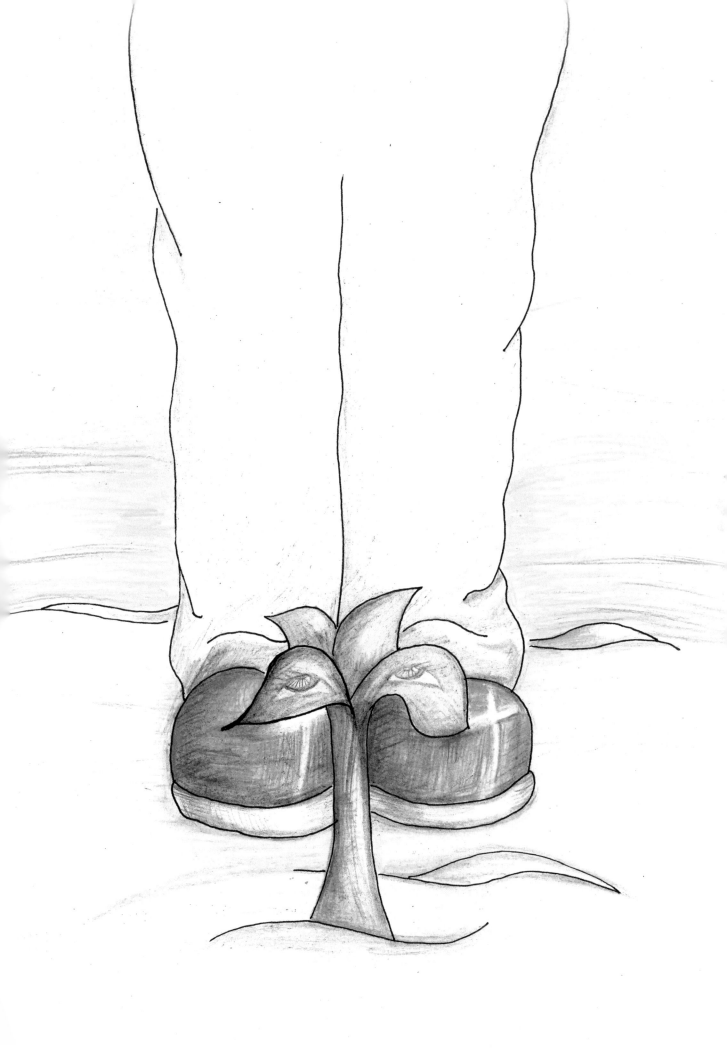

Without warning, she felt a pull. That pull was making her uncomfortable. The Gardener seemed to be loosening the dirt around her. This made no sense to her. She was doing fine! Why was he disturbing her now? What happened next was unimaginable. The Gardener pulled the plant from her dirt. She was more than uncomfortable. Now it hurt! He even shook the remaining dirt from her roots.

"How could you be doing this? Why now? Why me? I'm no weed!" she cried out to The Gardener. Yet she received no answers.

The Gardener then gently carried her away from everything that was familiar. Away from everything that seemed comfortable. Away from all the other plants she had grown secure with. Sure, she would sometimes wonder if life could be better, or at least something more, but that was all just a dream. She felt certain nothing that would happen next would be worth the pain, loneliness and confusion she was now feeling. Even more puzzling to her was that among the confusion and even anger she was feeling, deep inside she felt a small sense of hope. This made even less sense. From the view of all the other plants she had been living with, things looked hopeless for her.

Then, she looked upon the face of The Gardener.

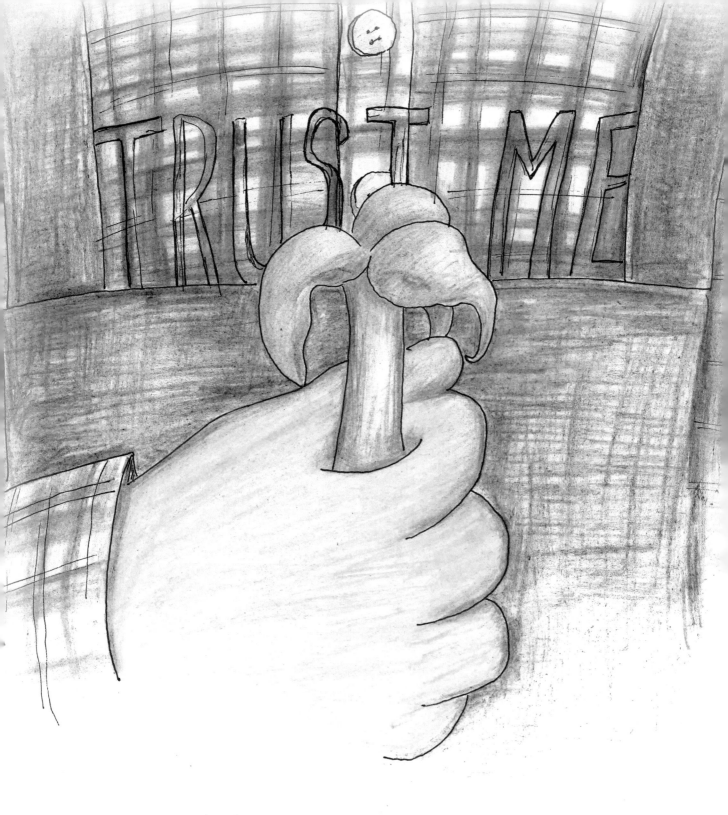

The Gardener was looking at her with such kindness, as if to say, "trust me". She felt fragile and wanted so badly for him to tell her where he was taking her. "If you would just let me know what is going to happen next, then I can trust you," the little plant screamed from her heart. The Gardener remained silent.

He took the plant on what seemed like a long journey. She felt so weak, as if she would never survive what was happening to her. When they arrived at the destination, The Gardener gently placed the plant on the ground and knelt beside her.

She could feel that he truly cared for her and saw the compassion
on his face. Being this close to him, she began to realize
that he was doing something good, even though she did not
know what it was. She softly whispered, "Thank you."

Suddenly, The Gardener picked her up and placed her
in new soil. This ground felt different. It felt better than
the dirt she was used to. As The Gardener patted the
soil around her roots, she began to feel comforted.

Next, he covered her with water that flowed freely around her and soaked the ground she lay in. "This is exactly what I needed!" she said to herself.

As time went by, night would come and then the sun would rise. The sun would then set to usher in yet another night. Again and again, another day would come and night would follow. Time was changing things in the life of the little plant.

She was now planted in a large field with other plants. Many of the other plants around her were stronger and larger. They would share stories of how The Gardener was always there with them, working and preparing their field. The plants were not all the same, but The Gardener seemed to be what they all had in common. She had never seen plants this strong and beautiful up close before. Their leaves shined, and they produced an abundance of fruit. She had heard stories of plants like these and often dreamed of being more like them. She remembered wanting to be cared for by The Gardener, and was now one of his treasured plants! How wonderful it was knowing she could be close to him and talk to him every day. In fact, she noticed it pleased him greatly, so began doing this more. The Gardener became her closest friend.

Day by day, she could tell her roots were becoming stronger and began to spread out underneath her.

On the surface, she also grew stronger. Her leaves became shiny, flowers bloomed all over her, and all the plants could see the changes. Then, one day, the plant heard the most surprising thing; someone called her a tree! She had known about other trees and how they lived to bear fruit for The Gardener. To her, they always seemed so happy. And on the day the first fruit began to grow on her branches, she knew the happiness too.

She remembered how she thought she was happy and content to produce just a few pretty flowers. How much more wonderful it was now to produce an abundance of fruit! Fruit that can be shared. Fruit that can feed others. Fruit that would please The Gardener.

She thought of the seeds in the middle of
the fruit. She then finally saw....

She was a seed, who only wanted to be a plant,
who was intended to be a tree...

And she would be.

Printed in the United States
By Bookmasters